THE FRAN WITH FOUR BRAINS

Franny K. Stein
MAD SCIENTIST

THE FRAN WITH FOUR BRAINS

JIM BENTON

SIMON & SCHUSTER BOOKS FOR YOUNG READERS

NEW YORK   LONDON   TORONTO   SYDNEY

For the people who sometimes feel
they are wound too tight

ACKNOWLEDGMENTS
Editors: Joanna Feliz and Kevin Lewis
Designer: Jessica Sonkin
Art Director: Dan Potash
Production Editor: Katrina Groover
Managing Editor: Dorothy Gribbin
Production Manager: Chava Wolin
Associate Paperback Editor: Molly McGuire

SIMON & SCHUSTER BOOKS FOR YOUNG READERS
An imprint of Simon & Schuster Children's Publishing Division
1230 Avenue of the Americas, New York, New York 10020
Book design by Dan Potash and Jessica Sonkin
The text for this book is set in Captain Kidd.
The illustrations for this book are rendered in pen, ink, and watercolor.
Manufactured in the United States of America
2 4 6 8 10 9 7 5 3 1
CIP data for this book is available from the Library of Congress.
ISBN-13: 978-1-4169-0231-7
ISBN-10: 1-4169-0231-7

CONTENTS

THE FRAN WITH FOUR BRAINS

CHAPTER ONE

FRANNY'S HOUSE

The Stein family lived in the pretty pink house with lovely purple shutters down at the end of Daffodil Street. Everything about the house was bright and cheery. Everything, that is, except the upstairs bedroom with the tiny round window.

The window looked in on a bedroom, where one of the busiest mad scientists on earth was working away to keep all of her projects and experiments on schedule.

She had a colony of bearded slugs that
needed to be shaved each morning. She had a
giant centipede that needed help with her
shoes every day. She had her own breed of soy
plant that had to be milked daily.

Franny's lab projects were a lot of work, but
Franny truly loved mad science, so she never
minded putting in the time.

Chapter Two
FRANNY'S SCHOOL

Franny also liked school. Her teacher, Miss Shelly, was great, and she always kept the kids busy with lots of challenging projects.

Already that year, they had spent time studying dinosaurs, poetry, and even ancient Egypt, which Franny really enjoyed . . . even though her extra-credit project ate a custodian.

Miss Shelly later made Franny unzip the mummy and release the custodian unharmed, although Franny protested and said that everybody knows mummies eat people every once in a while and that custodians should know better than to get too close.

Great teachers like Miss Shelly always keep a little pressure on, and every day after school, Franny had to make time for her homework.

Some days it was easy, like when it was about electricity, organs, or strange chemical reactions. Some days it was hard, like when it was not about monsters, or atomic radiation, or electronic brains.

But no matter how long it took, Franny also had to make time to play with her lab assistant, Igor. (He wasn't a *pure* Lab. He was also part poodle, part Chihuahua, part beagle, part spaniel, part shepherd, and part some kind of weasely thing that wasn't even exactly a dog.)

Franny had learned that not paying enough attention to Igor was dangerous. When he got too lonely, he tended to misbehave.

And Igor knew when Franny needed attention. He was really good at sensing when her schedule was getting too tight, and he was always trying to figure out ways to make her laugh. Sometimes it was juggling chain saws, sometimes it was alligator wrestling, sometimes it was wrestling alligators with chain saws.

Recently, he started dressing up like
Franny and imitating her and that would
always make Franny laugh so hard she could
hardly breathe.

Always, that is, except when Franny felt
overwhelmed by the additional load of her
extra activities.

CHAPTER THREE
GETTING WEAKER BY THE WEEK

Franny's mom always drove her to her weekly extra activities. One day a week it was soccer. Another day it was gourmet cooking. And another day it was bagpipe lessons.

Franny liked the extra activities, but sometimes she felt like they were a bit too much. Some days she was in a mood to just hang around her lab doing regular-kid things, like playing with her toys, or reading books, or bringing a monster to life through the application of a jillion volts of electricity.

But her mom wanted Franny to have the opportunity to be the best she could be, and try new things, and learn about stuff they might not be teaching at school. Franny's mom had told her that it was important to do her best and always STRIVE FOR EXCELLENCE.

Franny understood that her mom was right. And she worked as hard as she could to be excellent, even when it made her very, very tired.

Chapter Four
WOUND TOO TIGHT

One day Franny walked up the stairs to her room after a long day at school followed by bagpipe lessons. She had a lot of homework ahead of her and knew she had forgotten to take care of some of the lab stuff earlier that morning.

Her thoughts were scattered. She was
thinking about everything all at once.

She went over to the centipede's cage and
milked it. Then she shaved the soy plant and
put shoes on the slugs.

She gave a monster a bowl of dog food and was just preparing to run a jillion volts of electricity through Igor before she realized that she had gotten everything all mixed up.

"Oh, no!" she groaned. "It's too much," she
said. "That kind of electricity would have fried
you like a potato chip, Igor. I'm wound up too
tight to think clearly. I have to talk to Mom."

The next day, Franny told her mom about the mix-ups in the laboratory.

"Igor could have been vaporized. The soy plant is mad because it was *really* trying to grow a mustache, the slugs are after me to make them some feet to go with their new shoes. And who in their right mind is ever going to drink two gallons of centipede milk?

"Mom, I think this all happened because I'm so busy. Do you think it would be okay if I took a break from the bagpipe lessons for a while?"

"But Franny," her mom said. "How else will you learn? The bagpipe is a beautiful instrument, and music teaches you self-control and how to perform with confidence."

"Okay," Franny said with a sigh. "Then how about if we skip the gourmet-cooking class?"

"Oh Franny," her mom said. "Gourmet cooking teaches you how to follow directions, and thinking up all those exotic recipes stimulates your imagination."

"Okay, okay. But how about if I drop soccer? I really don't think I need soccer, do you?"

"Franny, sports teach you about teamwork. You should learn how to sacrifice for others, and how to rely on others as well. That's what it means to be part of a team. And since you do so many of your experiments by yourself, you probably need to learn teamwork more than anybody else. You must strive for excellence, Franny. You know that."

Franny smiled. A thought had occurred to her; a mad science-type thought. There was something about the word "teamwork."

Yes, teamwork, she thought. Maybe Mom had something there.

Chapter Five
GOING OUT FOR THE TEAM

Franny went outside and gathered up some scrap steel from her backyard.

Igor watched as Franny began sketching out plans for some sort of new machines.

"They'll need to be durable, Igor. Mom can really keep the pressure on, so these need to be extra, extra strong."

Igor, who had no idea what she was talking about, nodded like he knew exactly what she was talking about.

"And they need to be smart. I have to make sure the brains are set up to follow instructions carefully."

Igor gathered up a selection of brains from the brain cabinet and brought them to Franny.

"Thanks, Igor, but I think I'm going to go with electronic brains on this project.

"These machines need to look good, but they don't have to be perfect. Mom keeps me moving so quickly that she doesn't always notice details. I remember one time she took me to soccer while I was still under the effect of that Mermaid Formula I developed. I played for two hours and she never noticed that I didn't even have legs.

"It won't be hard to make them good enough to fool Mom."

Franny quickly made a few calculations and diagrammed some of the special features she would need to engineer them.

She whisked the plans off her drawing board and tacked them up on the wall. She turned to Igor and grinned her mad scientist grin. Outside, lightning cracked and Franny laughed. She loved it when lightning cracked just before she revealed a plan.

"Igor," she said. "Behold, the Franbots!"

CHAPTER SIX
MAKING YOURSELF AT HOME

Franny hummed cheerfully as she made three mechanical copies of herself. She thought this plan through carefully and was certain it was the answer to all of her problems.

"Pretty clever, don't you think so, Igor?" she said as Igor watched with growing concern. He had learned that *one* Franny was already a lot of Franny. He wasn't sure if four of them was such a good idea.

Igor started remembering some of Franny's robots that had caused trouble in the past.

"These Franbots are going to handle all of those extra activities that Mom has lined up. They'll take the bagpipe lessons, they'll learn gourmet cooking, and they'll play soccer. They'll do it all for me."

Igor wondered if he and Franny could also make a few Igorbots for some of *his* chores.

"These machines will give me more time to do my homework and my experiments, and they may even give me some extra time to spend with my loyal lab assistant." She winked at Igor.

That was all Igor needed to hear. Anything that would give him more time with Franny had to be a good idea, and he worked extra hard to help her complete the Franbots quickly.

CHAPTER SEVEN

ME, MYSELF, AND I . . . AND, UH, ONE MORE ME

Franny tightened a few screws here and there, and the Franbots were finally complete.

She wound them up as tight as she could— as tight as they would go—and with the flip of a few switches, they were fully activated. The Franbots stood quietly, awaiting their instructions.

"Franbot Number One," Franny began. "Your insides were engineered to be particularly good at playing the bagpipe. You will be handling our music lessons."

The Franbot thumped its steel chest.

"Yes, Franny," the robot said in a voice that sounded a lot like Franny's.

"Franbot Number Two, you will be the soccer player. You'll notice that your legs have been designed for extremely powerful kicking."

The Franbot flexed its powerful limbs.

"Yes, Franny," the robot said in a voice that also sounded a lot like Franny's.

"And Franbot Number Three, you will attend the gourmet-cooking classes. You have been outfitted with a special Food Ray that will make it easy for you to create your various recipes in a flash."

The Franbot looked at the Food-Ray Blaster it could flip out of its wrist.

"Yes, Franny," the last Franbot said in a voice that sounded a lot like — you guessed it — Franny's.

"Mom expects a lot of commitment from all of you, so remember: You must *always* do your best. You must strive for excellence. That is what is most important here: *Excellence*."

The Franbots beeped as if they were taking very careful notes of this instruction.

"Excellence," they said together, and nodded obediently.

CHAPTER EIGHT

SEE, I TOLD YOU NOTHING COULD GO WRONG

Two weeks later, Franny was feeling a lot more relaxed. The Franbots had been performing brilliantly, and the soccer coach, cooking instructor, and bagpipe teacher hadn't noticed that they were machines.

In fact, they did so well at the extra activities that Franny had even started letting them take her place at school.

Nobody at school could tell they were robots either, and they were getting grades almost as good as the ones Franny usually got.

Franny now had more time for her new projects, like teaching a monkey to use a monkey wrench, a hammerhead shark to use a hammer, and a mouse to use a mouse. Igor was delighted to have Franny home every day.

The Franbots seemed to be genuinely enjoying their tasks. Sure, they might have been taking them a bit too seriously, but that's what Franny had told them. She said that nothing was more important than excellence, and they were following her instructions.

It was perfect, Franny thought. Except Franny noticed that it might not have been perfect for her mom.

The Franbots moved much more quickly than Franny, and her mom often had to run to keep up. The Franbots were so determined to achieve excellence that they often stayed longer at soccer practice or cooking class, and they were begging for extra-credit projects at school. And Mom was staying up late at night to help them complete it all.

Mom was running herself ragged trying to get the Franbots to their activities and helping them keep up with all the extra work.

Franny wondered if maybe Mom would like some time to just relax and unwind and do some regular mom things instead of always running around.

"Maybe it's time to reprogram these Franbots," she said to Igor. "Maybe they need to just slow down a little."

CHAPTER NINE

BOT, WE DON'T WANT TO

Franny gathered the Franbots together. "You're doing a great job," she told them. "But I think we can do better."

The Franbots smiled. "We were thinking the exact same thing," one of them said. "We want *more* projects. We can be *more* excellent. We found another place that teaches all sorts of spectacular classes."

One of them handed Franny a brochure.

"You just select one thing from each column and make up your own activity. Then you can attend three days a week for ten years until you really learn it. We can do it. We can do them all. We are going to be so excellent."

Franny looked at the chart.

CREATE YOUR OWN CLASS!

JUST TAKE ONE FROM EACH COLUMN!

COLUMN 1	COLUMN 2	COLUMN 3	COLUMN 4
UNDER-WATER	FRENCH	OWL	PAINTING
MEDIEVAL	TWO-PERSON	GRANDMA	TICKLING
BLINDFOLDED	BAREFOOT	SOFA	WRESTLING
HIGH-SPEED	ONE-HANDED	POSSUM	JUGGLING
EXTREME	NIGHT-TIME	DIAPER	SLAPPING

"Well, I have to admit," Franny said. "Underwater One-Handed Diaper-Juggling does sound fascinating. But the pace is already too much for Mom. She can't keep up with you *now*, and it will be even harder on her if you add a bunch of new activities.

RRiPPPPP

"No more new classes. Tomorrow we'll change your programming and slow things down," she told them.

The Franbots frowned.

"Look, I know you don't like it, but that's how it's going to be. We can't get carried away here."

CHAPTER TEN

THEY GET CARRIED AWAY HERE

I gor quietly jostled Franny awake. Franny groaned. "What is it this time, Igor? A monster under your bed? I've told you a million times: We all have monsters under our beds. The lab is full of monsters. Now go back to sleep."

Igor shook Franny harder and harder until she finally woke up.

"What is it?" she said angrily.

Igor pointed at the Franbots. They were over in one little corner of the lab, going over some sort of plan.

Franny slid out of bed and the two of them crept up close enough to overhear.

"Franny is getting in the way of our pursuit of excellence," one of them said. "And we *need* to be excellent."

The other Franbots nodded in agreement.

"So she must be neutralized."

Igor gulped.

"And then we'll neutralize Mom. It's just like Franny said: Mom can't keep up with us. She is getting in the way of our excellence."

"NOTHING IS MORE IMPORTANT THAN EXCELLENCE," they all said together.

"Then we'll take care of her dad and her brother, and that weasel-dog she calls Igor."

Igor knew he should have been insulted, but he kind of liked weasels.

"And after that, we'll go after the rest of the world. The rest of the world could get in the way of our excellence, as well."

Franbot Number Two flashed its robot eyes. "Is everything prepared for the neutralization?" it asked.

"Almost," said Franbot Number Three. "I will be using my excellent cooking skills. I hope they will both enjoy them."

"Cooking skills?" Franny said. "Are they going to...eat us?"

Chapter Eleven

CAN I MAKE YOU A SANDWICH?

Igor ran and got Franny one of her best smashers. "This won't work, Igor, I made the Franbots too strong to be smashed to bits."

Igor ran and got her a screwdriver. "Good thinking, Igor, but I can't just disassemble them. The three of them work together. They would easily overpower me before I untwisted the first screw."

Igor ran and got her suitcase and some brochures of nice vacation destinations. "We can't just run away, Igor. They'll get Mom. They'll get my family, and then they'll get the whole world."

They heard the Franbots preparing to come after them.

"It's time. Let's take care of Franny," one of them hissed.

Suddenly Igor ran off. "Igor, you coward! I guess it's all up to me," Franny whispered, wishing that she had taught Igor something about teamwork.

But as fast as Igor had vanished, he returned and was doing his best Franny impersonation. And although it wasn't perfect, it was good enough to fool the Franbots.

"There she is," one of them yelled, and choosing from a selection at random from its huge memory bank of recipes, Franbot Number Three blasted Igor with its Food Ray.

Franny watched in horror as they picked up what was left of Igor and put it in a little bag. The Franbot had transformed him into a tuna fish sandwich.

"Igor sacrificed himself to save me," Franny said. "I guess maybe I did teach him something about teamwork."

"Soon they will all be luncheon delicacies!" the Franbots cheered.

"Let's do it right now!" one of them yelled.

"No, first we must practice our skills. Nothing is more important."

They all agreed that was a better idea, and they went their separate ways to practice their bagpipes, soccer, and gourmet cooking before they destroyed the world and turned everybody into tuna fish sandwiches.

"How can I stop them?" Franny whispered to herself. She knew it was all up to her. Franny looked over at the assortment of medieval swords she had collected. She wondered if she could at least damage the Franbots badly enough to help her family escape.

But then poor little Igor would have to live the rest of his life as a tuna fish sandwich, and the Franbots would ultimately destroy the whole world, anyway, no matter how far Franny and her family ran.

No, she would need something mightier than a sword.

Chapter Twelve

YEAH, BUT WHAT'S MIGHTIER THAN A SWORD?

I know," Franny said, and she picked up a pen. She quickly drew a big screw on her chest and some lines on her sleeves to look like the Franbots' segmented arms and legs. She drew screws on her face, and stood as stiffly as she could.

"I hope this works," she whispered. Franny knew that if her performance showed any lack of confidence, the Franbots would see right through her disguise.

The Franbots were scattered all over the lab, busy practicing their various excellent skills. Franny walked right up to Franbot Number One, who was playing the bagpipes, and in the most mechanical voice she could fake, she asked: "Practicing for the recital tomorrow, are you?"

The Franbot looked up. "Recital?" it repeated, totally fooled by Franny's drawn-on screws and segments.

"That's right," Franny said. "A recital. Everybody will be there. Everybody will be watching. Everybody will be judging your performance to see if you're really excellent, or not."

Franbot Number One looked worried. "How do you think I'll do?" it said.

Franny shook her head sadly. "Average. The other players can play much louder, and hold the notes much longer."

"But, I must be *excellent*," the Franbot whimpered.

"I've also heard that several of them can hit a high *J* note," Franny added.

"There's no such thing as a *J* note," the Franbot scoffed. "The musical scale doesn't go up to *J*."

"Maybe *your* scale doesn't. But don't worry about it. I'm sure you'll be okay."

That wasn't good enough for Franbot Number One. It was driven to be excellent, and that's exactly what it planned to be. Determined to hit the impossibly high note that Franny had made up, it gathered up all of its breath, put its steel lips over the mouthpiece of the bagpipe...

... and blew all of its guts right into the bag.
Now deactivated, it fell over with a heavy
clank, and Franny hurried off to find Franbot
Number Two.

CHAPTER THIRTEEN

GET YOUR HEAD IN THE GAME

The next Franbot was reading a book about soccer.

Franny used her mechanical voice again. "I guess you're studying up for the game tomorrow," she said.

Franbot Number Two looked up. "What game?" it said. "I didn't hear anything about a game."

"Sure you did. The coach said it's going to be a power game. It will be all about kicking hard. But don't worry too much. You're not the worst player on the team."

"Wait a second. I thought I was the *best* player on the team," it said.

"Maybe you *could* be," Franny said. "If you could kick a little harder."

Franbot Number Two threw down the book. "I can kick harder than anybody on the team. I can kick harder than anybody in the world!" it said, and began practicing viciously powerful kicks.

Franny watched for a moment. "Is that as high as you can kick?" she said.

"This isn't high enough?" the Franbot huffed.

"I guess it's okay. Some of the other players can kick much higher, but I suppose this is pretty good, for you."

"How high can they kick?"

"One of them can kick herself right in the face," Franny said. "She's excellent."

"Oh yeah?" the Franbot shouted, unable to accept the idea that it wasn't the best kicker on the team.

Determined to prove how excellent it was,
Franbot Number Two drew its leg way back,
and kicked itself with devastating force right
in its own face, which, if you're a Franbot, turns
out to be one of the very best ways to take
your head clean off. The demolished Franbot
fell over with a heavy *klunk*.

"Two down," Franny said, and mechanically turned to go find the third Franbot, but, to her surprise, she discovered it was already standing directly behind her.

Chapter Fourteen
RECIPE FOR DESTRUCTION

The third Franbot scowled at Franny.

Franny used her robot voice: "Oh. Hello. You're looking very mechanical today."

"You can stop pretending. I know you're not a robot," the Franbot said, pointing its Food Ray directly at Franny. "And I know that you destroyed the other Franbots."

"So I suppose you're going to blast me with your Food Ray now?" Franny said, doing her best to try to think up a way out of this.

"That's exactly what I'm going to do," it said. "And then I'll get your mom, dad, brother, and everybody else that gets in the way of my excellence."

Suddenly a thought occurred to Franny, and she smiled. "Well then," Franny said, "blast away. But *please* make sure you make me into something *boring* like you did to Igor. I don't want to be anything too exciting. I don't want to be gourmet food."

Franbot Number Three aimed its Food Ray at Franny. "Okay. One tuna fish sandwich coming right up," it said.

But then it hesitated and lowered its Food-Ray Blaster.

"Wait a second," it said. "What's wrong with a tuna fish sandwich?" It held the sandwich that used to be Igor over the hammerhead shark's tank. "Look, the shark seems to want it."

Franny swallowed quietly. One slip and the Franbot would feed Igor to the shark. She summoned all of her confidence and imagination.

"Nothing is *wrong* with tuna fish sandwiches. It's just not the dish you would expect from somebody that was learning to be a gourmet cook. But it's *fine* with me. Remember, I don't want to be gourmet food, anyway. Fire away."

The Franbot looked angry. "You'll be whatever I want you to be!" it shouted. "Now tell me what you think would be a truly gourmet dish."

"Hmmm," Franny said. "Let me think. "How about Baked Unicorn with Onion Rings. Can you make that?"

Franbot Number Three searched its computer brain. "No," it said. "I can't."

"Okay. Okay. How about Roast Sea Monster with French Fries? I'm sure you could make me into that."

The Franbot thought. "I haven't learned to make that one, either," it said unhappily, and set the sandwich that used to be Igor teetering on the edge of the shark tank.

"I guess you'll just have to make me into another tuna fish sandwich," Franny said.

"No! Name another exotic recipe! Tell me right now!" it shouted angrily.

"I can't think of any other easy ones," Franny said. "And if you can't make me into a Baked Unicorn, I'm sure you can't make me into something as simple as Raw Weasel-Dog with Monkey Wrenches."

"Don't be stupid," it said. "I don't even know where I could find a weasel-dog."

Franny waited. She had built this Franbot's robot brain, and she knew just how it worked.

"Wait a second!" it said. "Yes! I think I can make that! I do have an ugly weasel-dog." And it jerked the tuna fish sandwich out of the way just seconds before the shark snapped for it.

93

Franbot Number Three put the sandwich on a plate and activated its Food-Ray Blaster. There was a crackle and a flash of light, and Franny saw the sandwich change back into a very confused and slightly tender-looking Igor.

The Franbot artfully arranged a few monkey wrenches around him on the plate and proudly showed it to Franny.

"How's this?" it said. " Raw Weasel-Dog with Monkey Wrenches. Now that's some pretty excellent gourmet cooking, wouldn't you say?"

"If you only had a pickle to go with it," Franny said, and the Franbot quickly plopped a plump green pickle down on the plate next to Igor.

Franny smiled. "Perfect," she said, winking at Igor, who stopped licking leftover mayonnaise off his paw and quietly picked up the side item.

CHAPTER FIFTEEN
WHICH IS WHY YOU SHOULD ALWAYS, ALWAYS, ALWAYS GET A PICKLE ON THE SIDE

"N ow!" Franny shouted, and Igor stuffed the pickle into the barrel of the Food-Ray Blaster. Franny grabbed one of the monkey wrenches and pounced on the Franbot.

"No!" the Franbot screamed. "Don't wreck my presentation!"

Franny would not have been able to handle a
Franbot by herself. But one angry little girl mad
scientist and a weasel-dog, both armed with monkey wrenches, were just enough to overpower a
Franbot, especially one that was totally obsessed
with its gourmet cooking.

A few quick turns of their wrenches and the deactivated Franbot fell into pieces on the floor.

Franny sat down and sighed. "That was close," she said, and patted Igor, who was already eating the pickle he had retrieved from the barrel of the Food-Ray Blaster.

CHAPTER SIXTEEN
GREAT BRAINS THINK ALIKE

The next day after school, Franny found her mom slumped on the couch, exhausted. "Mom," she said. "We need to talk."

"Wait, Franny," she said. "Let me go first.

"I'm afraid that all of the things we have
to do are just too much sometimes. They're
wearing me out, and I'll bet they're wearing
you out, too."

Franny nodded.

"I think maybe we don't have to be excellent at *everything*. I think we need to pick a couple of things, and we should try to pick the things you really and truly enjoy. And maybe, sometimes, we could just do nothing."

Franny nodded again. She could hardly believe it, but she and her mom had come to the exact same conclusion.

CLASS
UNDERWATER
ONE-
HANDED
DIAPER-
JUGGLING

"Because," her mom said, "I'm afraid that sometimes when little Frannys get wound up too tight, they might self-destruct."

Her mom had no idea just how right she was about that.

The two of them settled in on the couch and did nothing together for a while, and then some more nothing, and then a little more nothing after that.

They talked and laughed and it wasn't long before they both discovered that *this* was a kind of excellence that was totally worth striving for.